MAGIC
at the BED & BISCUIT

Joan Carris

illustrated by Noah Z. Jones

CANDLEWICK PRESS

Text copyright © 2011 by Joan Carris
Illustrations copyright © 2011 by Noah Z. Jones

First paperback edition 2011

The Library of Congress has cataloged the hardcover edition as follows:

Carris, Joan Davenport.
Magic at the Bed and Biscuit / Joan Carris ; illustrated by Noah Z. Jones. — 1st ed.
p. cm.
Summary: The family of animals at the Bed and Biscuit are expected to welcome and help protect Malicia, a mean-spirited city chicken who tours with a magic show, but all are afraid of her temper and powers.
ISBN 978-0-7636-4306-5 (hardcover)
[1. Veterinarians — Fiction. 2. Animals — Fiction. 3. Magic — Fiction.]
I. Jones, Noah (Noah Z.) ill. II. Title.
PZ7.C2347Mag 2010
[Fic] — dc22   2009047409

ISBN 978-0-7636-5849-6 (paperback)

12 13 14 15 16 17 RRC 10 9 8 7 6 5 4 3 2 1

Printed in Crawfordsville, IN, U.S.A.

This book was typeset in Old Claude.
The illustrations were done in pencil and watercolor.

Candlewick Press
99 Dover Street
Somerville, Massachusetts 02144

visit us at www.candlewick.com

For Andrea and Mary Lee, for many reasons
J. C.

For Sylvie and Eli
N. Z. J.

Contents

A Dinky Chicken 1

Poor Rory 11

Malicia Teaches Another Lesson 23

Meet Me in the Tack Room 33

That's a Chicken for You 43

The Doo Incident 53

Don't Make Her Mad 67

Poor Professor Pig 77

So Many Stars 83

A Power Outage 93

Author's Note 101

1
A Dinky Chicken

"WHAT HAVE WE HERE?" asked Gabby the mynah bird. She eyed the newest guest at the Bed and Biscuit boardinghouse. "Are you some kind of dinky chicken?"

The tiny bird in the cage fluffed her silvery feathers and jabbed her dainty black beak at Gabby. "Are you some kind of fat-beaked parrot?"

"I'm a Vietnamese hill mynah, you twerp!" Gabby waved her huge orange beak in the air for emphasis.

"Now, now," Ernest said in a soothing tone, "we need to get along." *Even with chickens,* he thought gloomily. Normally a thoughtful and open-minded mini-pig, Ernest detested chickens.

"I can't thank you enough for taking my chicken," Barnabas told Grampa. "I think she's healthy but really tired. We've just come off a long tour, and I know *I'm* tired. Moving a large magic show from city to city is exhausting."

"Of course," Grampa said. "Please, Barnabas, sit down. I made egg-salad sandwiches and fresh coffee."

Over supper, they visited. "I used to have Silkie bantams like yours," Grampa said. "I let them roam so they could eat bugs. Great protein

in bugs! I plan to do the same with your chicken, but don't worry — my whole family will keep an eye on her."

"Your family?" Barnabas asked.

"They're part of the system. My pig, Ernest, really runs the place. He has a better snout than any dog, and he helps with chores." Grampa scratched Ernest behind his ears. "Gabby chats with our boarders to amuse them, and my cat, Milly, purrs people to sleep . . . or licks them clean. My puppy, Sir Walter, makes everyone laugh — especially me."

As if called, Sir Walter the Scottie burst into the kitchen by way of the pet door. Milly followed at a sedate, ladylike pace.

Grampa lifted the chicken's cage off the floor and set it on the table. When Milly got up in his lap to peer into the cage, Grampa held on to her. "Don't frighten the little chicken, Milly. She doesn't know you won't hurt her. Isn't she cute? Her name is Malicia, and she'll be with us for a while until she's rested up." He gave Milly a chance to examine Malicia, then set his cat back on the floor.

"Yarp, yarp!" shrilled the puppy, pawing at Grampa's pant leg.

"Okay, okay," said Grampa, picking him up. "See, Sir Walter? It's a teeny little chicken. And there'll be no chasing her, laddie, hear me?" He held the puppy up to his face and said again, "No chasing this birdie, okay?"

Sir Walter whimpered and craned his head around to look at Malicia. "Yarp?" he went again, straining toward the cage.

Barnabas said, "You'll have to keep an eye on him, Adam. He'd dearly love to chase my chicken."

"Yup, but Ernest and Milly won't let him. I told you, I have a system here and it works! My family will guard Malicia. I will, too, of course. I don't want to think of you on vacation, all stressed out about your chicken!" Grampa paused, then said, "Just for the record, how old is she? It'll make a difference in what I feed her."

"Let's see. She got star billing in Dad's act for about twenty years, along with our rabbit, Houdini. After Houdini died, Dad retired and I took over, about fifteen years ago. So she's almost forty, and I doubt that I can replace her! That's why you've got her. You're one of my oldest friends, besides being my favorite vet. I trust you completely." Barnabas took the last sandwich.

"She's almost forty," Grampa repeated slowly. "Yes, I am a veterinarian, but I have never heard of a forty-year-old chicken!" He shook his head and went for another cup of coffee.

"But this is a magic chicken! I warned you about that already. She can be a real handful, and lately she's been quite difficult."

Grampa let out a big breath. He put his glasses on the table, drank a sip of coffee, then said, "Look, Barnabas, our families have been friends for years, and I'm honored that you trust me with your antique chicken, but I'm a normal guy. I will do my very best in all ways, but —"

"I know, I know," Barnabas hastened to say. "I just wanted you to understand how important Malicia is to me."

"Oh, I understand! Everyone who boards an animal here feels the same way. So do I! And I am looking forward to spoiling your chicken."

Grampa picked up Malicia's cage and held it close to his face so he could look Malicia in the eye. "Not to worry, little chickabiddy. I love Silkies."

Zap! Malicia nailed his nose with her teeny, sharp beak.

"Yow!" cried Grampa, setting the cage back on

the table. He put one finger up to soothe his nose. "Would you look at that! She drew blood!"

"YARP! YARP! YARP!" Sir Walter bounced up and down with the effort of barking.

"BAD CHICKEN! BAAAAD CHICKEN!" shrieked Gabby, who had flown to Grampa's shoulder and was rubbing her beak gently on his cheek.

"OINK! OINK! OINK!" Ernest grunted over and over.

"MROWRRR! FFFTTT! SSSSTTT!" went Milly.

While Grampa put a wet cloth to his nose, Barnabas moved Malicia's cage to his lap. "Oooh, bad baby," Barnabas said tenderly. He made a soft *tsk-tsk* sound. "Dr. Bender's animals will show you the beautiful country here, sweetie. And he'll give you the tastiest food you ever ate. You can sleep all you want and hunt bugs in real grass. Then Papa will come get you, okay?"

Malicia gave him a stony stare.

Grampa rolled his eyes and went for yet another cup of coffee.

"Just be firm with her, Adam, and you won't have any trouble."

"Aw, phooey, Barnabas. She's going to love it here!" Grampa replied.

Ernest nodded his head toward his bed in the kitchen corner, and the other animals knew to join him there. Gabby took her customary place in the center of Ernest's pile of blankets. "Did you hear that?" she asked Milly, who lounged on Ernest's blue pillow. "She's a magic chicken, whatever that is."

"Ffftt," Milly replied. "Mainly she's rude."

"Mean, too," added Sir Walter. "Why did she bite Grampa?"

"I have no idea," Ernest said, "but you should avoid that chicken. She's a city chicken — not used to puppies — and she's hot-tempered."

Gabby quivered from the tip of her magnificent orange beak to the last purple-green tail feather. "This is just peachy! So far we have rude, mean, and hot-tempered."

"And we haven't even seen her magic yet!" Milly added.

2
Poor Rory

AFTER SETTLING MALICIA on her perch by a kitchen window, Barnabas left, promising to check in often with Grampa.

"Okay, old lady," Grampa told Malicia, "be sure you do your business on these papers. And don't give me that blank stare. If you're a magic chicken, you understand every word I'm saying." He picked up Milly, and the two went upstairs for the night as usual.

Gabby roosted on her curtain rod over the window beside the door.

Sir Walter settled himself against Ernest's stomach. "I have to sleep with you, Ernest. I'm afraid of that mean chicken."

Oh, well, he's still a baby, Ernest thought, moving to make room for the puppy. Wood snapped in the huge old iron stove, while the clock above it gave off a faint glow. Lulled by these familiar things, Gabby, Ernest, and the puppy fell asleep right away.

Four — maybe only three — peaceful minutes passed.

"It's very dark outside!" Malicia said. She had a penetrating voice.

Half asleep, Ernest raised his head. "This is the country. It's always dark at night here. It's good for sleeping," he added as a hint.

Malicia shifted on her perch. "It's very quiet, too!"

"Not quiet enough!" Gabby said.

"Everything is strange here," Malicia whined.

Wearily Ernest sat up. "This is the most wonderful room I know," he said. "It's much better than being in the barn with the other chickens or in the aviary with the birds who are boarding. We're lucky to be sleeping in a warm house."

"I don't care!" said Malicia. "Our apartment in the city is much nicer."

"I'm sure," Ernest said hastily, before Gabby could start an argument. "But give us a chance here! And now we must be quiet, or we'll be put out in the cold barn." That had never happened, but Ernest would have said anything to quiet Malicia. "Just think about running in the grass tomorrow, hunting bugs in the sun," he went on. "Crunchy crickets and squishy caterpillars, yum!"

"Yuck!" Sir Walter said.

"SILENCE!" boomed Ernest. He glared fiercely around the kitchen, which was now as quiet as the inside of a pillow. It stayed that way the rest of the night, too.

* * *

"Racka, racka, ROOO!" crowed Rory, as he had every dawn for the past five years. "Racka, RACKA, ROOOO! RACKA, RACKA, ROOOOO!"

Teeny black feet stalked across the kitchen and up onto Ernest's pile of blankets. "What is that unholy racket?" she screeched in his ear.

Ernest woke with a *snorrrt!* He looked around groggily for the strange voice, and then he remembered. "Malicia?" He sat up, saw her tiny, sharp beak, and inched back into the corner. He knew how much that beak would hurt his sensitive snout.

"I said —" began Malicia.

Gabby swooped in, landing next to Malicia with an impressive display of purple-green feathers. "That 'unholy racket' is morning in the country. Last night you said it was too quiet here!" Gabby clacked her beak.

"Now, now," said Ernest. He had no idea what to say next. From under his pillow came a low, puppy whimper.

"I do NOT like noise this early!" Malicia yelled. "I'm supposed to be resting, and I prefer rising at noon. That's what we do at home!"

"Shhh," Ernest whispered. "We keep quiet until Grampa gets up. He's old and needs his sleep."

Malicia waved a wing at the door. "But out there, that obnoxious —"

"That's our rooster, Rory. It's his job to crow at dawn. We're so used to him, we hardly hear him."

"Well, I'll tell him a thing or two," said Malicia. "Where is he?"

"You go, girl!" urged Gabby, who had often been bullied by Rory, an extra-large, extra-fierce Rhode Island Red. "He's never met a real city chicken!"

Malicia gave a shrill chirp and vanished. *Poof.* Gone.

"Yipe!" went Sir Walter. "Did you see that?"

Ernest had seen it but couldn't quite believe it. One second Malicia had been with them,

the next second — after only a tiny chirp — she had disappeared. He thought hard. "Well . . . I mean . . . for corn's sake! I wonder if she can vanish whenever she wants."

Dazed, they all sat very still. Gabby said, "It looks like she's really a magic chicken."

"An *evil* magic chicken," Sir Walter said firmly.

"Well, if she is," Gabby went on, sounding more cheerful, "then she won't have any trouble with Rory."

By six thirty that morning, when Grampa and Milly came downstairs, Ernest was sick of worrying alone while Gabby and the puppy slept. *"Psst,* Milly," he called.

Yawning, Milly ambled his way. After hearing that Malicia had vanished before their eyes, she said, "This is terrible! Grampa told Barnabas we'd watch out for her! How can we do that if she starts disappearing? I wish I'd never heard of her!"

"I know," Ernest said vaguely. He was still adjusting to the idea of an animal that could disappear at will. No self-respecting pig would ever behave that way.

"Come on, troops," Grampa said to Ernest, Milly, and the puppy. "Those cows are calling us."

In the next hour, Ernest took the heavy pails of fresh milk to the house, one by one — carrying them slowly in his strong jaws, setting them down gently on the porch. On his last trip to the house, Grampa and Sir Walter were with him. Grampa was carrying a jittery Sir Walter.

Grampa got busy separating the cream from the milk while Ernest, Milly, and Sir Walter sat on Ernest's bed and waited for their breakfast.

"I saw her near the barn," Sir Walter said. "I saw Malicia. She—"

"Eeep?" went Malicia as she appeared out of nowhere, mincing across the kitchen. "You called?"

"Yipe!" shrilled the puppy as he scurried behind Ernest.

Shaken, Ernest said, "We didn't call . . . exactly. But here you are." Ernest knew now that he did not like magic. It was unnerving.

Malicia climbed to the top of the blanket pile and settled exactly in the center, in Gabby's place.

Gabby flew down from her curtain rod and sat beside Ernest. She glared at Malicia but said nothing.

"Well . . . do you want to hear about my meeting with Rory or not?" asked Malicia.

"Please tell us," Ernest said, steeling himself for the worst.

"I went straight to the point. I explained who I am, and that I've just come off an absolutely exhausting tour. I must get my rest! I told him that this is a horribly boring place for a city show bird like me, but, sadly, I am here. Thus, he must not make a sound before noon, which is when I am accustomed to rising."

Gabby leaned forward. "What happened then?"

"Well! He just crowed in my face! So I removed some of his tail feathers to prove I meant business!"

"Removed some tail feathers? REMOVED?" oinked Ernest, growing more distraught by the second.

Gabby said, "Oooh, that's mean. Without tail feathers he can barely fly. I'm not a fan of Rory's, but you should put those feathers back."

"Forget it," Malicia replied. "I made them vanish. He should have done what I told him to do. He'll pay attention the next time."

Sir Walter sat down quickly on his black furry tail. He gave Milly a look, and she sat on her tail, too. Gabby stuck her colorful tail feathers under Ernest's right haunch, and all of them eyed Malicia fearfully.

3
Malicia Teaches Another Lesson

BY EIGHT THAT MORNING, Grampa had fixed breakfast for his family. Like all farm breakfasts, it was a hearty meal. Grampa and Ernest got eggs, fried potatoes, toast, and grits — lots of grits for Ernest. Gabby had yogurt and mixed fruit. Milly ate kitten kibbles, because she was still only ten months old, and the puppy got a special mixture of hamburger and yogurt.

"Come on, little old lady," Grampa said to Malicia. He took her to the porch, where he set out a pan of poultry feed with extra minerals and vitamins. "If you're like other chickens, this food will be all over the property by the time you're finished, so you eat outdoors."

In the kitchen, Milly groomed her spotless white bib, stomach, and paws. Sir Walter finished eating and attached himself to Ernest's left flank.

"Just relax," Ernest told him. "If you don't bother her, she won't bother you. She's a puny little chicken!"

"But she's a magic chicken!" Milly said, pausing in her grooming ritual. "Think about poor Rory."

Gabby looked up from crumb-hunting. "Milly and Sir Walter are right! It's only a matter of time before she picks on all of us. You wait and see! She is one nasty chicken!"

"Oh, for corn's sake!" Ernest cried. "We know that. But she's a guest, and Grampa promised his friend we would watch over her, remember?"

"Ah, it's Mr. Porky Professor again!" Gabby said. "Stop lecturing and tell us what you think we should do." She squawked rudely.

"Goodness," Grampa said. "What's all this ruckus? You folks haven't jawed at each other like this in ages." He knelt down beside Ernest's bed and petted each member of his family. "So how are you all doing with Malicia?"

"Eeep?" Malicia appeared instantly in their midst.

"Holy Toledo!" Grampa cried.

The puppy clawed at Grampa's chest, trying to get into the pocket on his shirt. Frowning in thought, Grampa picked him up, sat down on the floor, and focused on Malicia, who had again claimed the center of Ernest's bed. "Well," Grampa said to her, "you're going to be a handful, just like Barnabas said. Good thing I have only a few boarders this week."

He stood and opened the door to the porch. "Okay, everybody, now listen up! We all have to get along so I can get my work done!" Here he gave Malicia a stern look. "No more arguing. Go outside, show Malicia what a great place this is, and behave yourselves. This is a perfect Indian summer day!"

"Wrunk," Ernest said, happy to be going outdoors. With a confident trot he led everyone to the middle pasture, where the cows were. Cows meant manure, and manure meant bugs.

He showed Malicia a large brown blob of manure on the ground. "This is called a cow pie," he told her. "Pie is a treat, you know, and these old cow pies are full of delicious bugs. See that big, fat grub?"

Malicia quickly stabbed the fat white larva with her beak.

Gabby made the sound of someone throwing up. "I'll just sit over there in that nice apple tree," she said, taking flight.

Milly and Sir Walter began edging away, farther and farther. Milly called out, "Sir Walter wanted to chase the cows, but I said no. We'll just have a few races over here."

"That's good!" Ernest replied. By this time his sensitive snout was smarting from the pungent odor of the cow pies, and he was feeling sorry for himself. *I always have to be the responsible one,* he thought. *Mr. Dependable. Why is that?*

Opal, Pearl, and Ruby moseyed over to greet Ernest. "Is this a new boarder?" Ruby asked. "She's awfully small to be out here, isn't she?"

Malicia looked up from bug hunting and went, "Chip, chip!" in a most snooty manner. "Are they cows?" she asked Ernest.

"Yes, all three of them are Holstein cows. They give delicious milk twice a day. Grampa's neighbors buy our milk every week."

"You don't say," said Malicia. She flew up to the fence to get closer to Ruby's face and said, "What do you charge for your milk? What percentage are you earning?"

Ruby batted her long eyelashes. She looked at Pearl and Opal, who batted their eyelashes back at her. "Percentage? What are you talking about?"

"I might have known. Absolute country bumpkins. Do you work for *free,* then?"

"Cows do not work," Ruby said flatly. "We enjoy Grampa's three rich pastures, his warm barn in the winter, and each other's company. In turn, we give milk. We do not sell it. What a silly idea."

"Are you calling me silly?" Malicia shook with anger.

"If the word fits," replied Opal, who had always had a big mouth.

"More bugs over here!" cried Ernest, hoping to distract Malicia.

Feathers still aquiver, Malicia said, "I am a guest here, and you should not talk to me that way. Pay attention, and stop switching your tails around!"

Malicia waved her tiny wings in the air, creating miniature silver stars. Instantly the cows' tails stopped moving. They stuck straight out and looked purely ridiculous.

Appalled, Ernest looked from the cows to Malicia and back at the cows again. *That evil chicken has put a spell on their tails!* he thought. *This isn't regular magic. This is very* bad *magic.*

Malicia went into fits of chicken laughter. "Chip! Chip! Chip!" She was so pleased with herself that she rolled on the ground.

Meanwhile, large green flies began biting the cows.

"Please, Miss Chicken," Pearl begged, "please let us move our tails! We use them to keep the flies away!"

Ernest's eyes glowed with fury. "Ma-lish-AH!" he began.

"Oh, very well. But you have to admit they were rude. I was merely asking a business question." She waved one tiny wing at the cows, and their tails began thrashing back and forth, chasing away the cruel flies.

Malicia laughed again. "That was funny, wasn't it?"

Ernest shook his head no. He felt sorry for the gentle, generous cows who never harmed anyone. Worse, he was now afraid for his family. *What chance do we have against this evil chicken?*

4
Meet Me in the Tack Room

AT THE BED AND BISCUIT, the hour after lunch was nap time. Grampa took Milly and Sir Walter into the family room, where they slept together on the brown corduroy sofa. Gabby dozed on her curtain rod, and Ernest stretched out on his own bed. This was normally Ernest's favorite part of the day.

Not today. Instead, he was stewing over what had happened that morning. As he lay awake, he heard Malicia shifting around on her perch. "It is so boring here, I could just scream!" she said.

Ernest thought, *I have never liked a single chicken, but this one is the worst.* He pretended to snore.

"AWWK!" Malicia screamed, followed by her cackle, "Chip, chip! Oh, that is funny. I said it was so boring here, I could just scream, and then I—"

"Awwk! I could just *scream*," Gabby broke in, making Malicia sound like the sappiest chicken on earth. "I am *so* funny," Gabby continued. "I could just scream. Awwwk! Chip, chip—"

Silence.

Ernest opened his eyes and saw tiny silver stars around Malicia. Gabby sat on her perch with her beak wide open—very wide open and very still. Ernest hadn't seen a frozen mynah bird before, but he was seeing one now.

Malicia strikes again! thought Ernest, awed by her power. He rose to his feet, but before he could say anything, Malicia cut in. "That mangy old parrot was making fun of me. That is no way to treat a guest, and I won't have it, Ernest, so save your breath. I simply won't have it!"

"I see that," Ernest said, proud of how calm he sounded. He itched to sit on Malicia and squash her, or demand that she restore Gabby to normal, but he felt sure that both actions would backfire. *I'm acting a part,* he told himself. *I am being the Genial Host, while I wait for a chance to fix you, you wretched, evil chicken.*

"What can we do now?" Malicia asked pertly. "I am bored."

"Let's go outside," Ernest suggested smoothly. "We have so many places you haven't seen. I'll tell Milly and then we'll go." He trotted into the family room and quietly told Milly and Sir Walter, "Important meeting in the tack room right after naps. Tell Gabby."

On their way out, Ernest said, "Oh, uh, do me a favor, Malicia. I'm sure Gabby has learned her lesson by now, so please unfreeze her."

"Why? I prefer her to be quiet."

"Maybe, but great magicians never waste their talent on small magic. If they do, the talent goes away." He paused at the door, waiting. *What brilliant lines,* he thought. *Sometimes I amaze myself.*

Malicia hesitated, then waved a wing at Gabby, who jerked and nearly pitched off her curtain rod. She gazed warily down at Malicia and Ernest, but said nothing.

Outside, Ernest showed Malicia their stone barbecue grill that Grampa had built himself, Gramma's flower beds still bravely blooming, and the pond beside the barn. Malicia took a dirt bath near the barn, while Ernest watched and stoked his anger. *I don't know how we're going to do it, you rotten, evil chicken, but we're going to get you,* he promised himself. *You think you can get mad. Hah! You've never seen a mad pig!*

Malicia shook the fine dirt out of her feathers. "Lovely! Now what should we do?"

Ernest had a ready answer. "The far pasture," he said. "It's beautiful in the fall, and it has lots of old cow pies. Great bug territory."

"Fine," she said, flitting up to his head. "I'll ride on your head, the way Gabby does."

Ernest controlled his temper with effort. "Okay, but no claws. That's the rule."

Malicia rode happily all the way to the far pasture, where the maples glowed orange, yellow, and red in the autumn sun. Here the land rolled gently, creating low hills. Ernest stopped near the gate, in an area marked with old cow pies.

"Oh, yummy," Malicia said, fluttering to the ground. "The cow pies are my favorite part of the Bed and Biscuit."

"Happy to oblige," said Ernest the Genial Host. "Enjoy yourself. I'll just doze over here." He moved as far from the cow pies as possible, where he could still keep an eye on Malicia. He wouldn't doze, of course, though he still mourned his lost nap. *This spoiled, evil chicken has ruined every part of my life,* he thought.

When Ernest decided that nap time back at the house must be over, he stood up, pretended to yawn, and said, "I'm just going over the hill for a drink at the cold spring. I'll be back. Take your time."

Malicia barely looked up as Ernest jogged casually over the hill and out of sight. There he broke into a run, circled around the back way, and ended up at the barn. He flopped down gratefully in the dim, cool tack room, where Grampa kept bins of feed, apples, squash, potatoes, and sometimes pears for Gabby. The fragrant leather saddles were here, too, along with several tools.

Ernest was munching his third apple when Gabby, Milly, and Sir Walter arrived. "What's up?" Milly asked.

"We need to talk about you-know-who. And don't say her name!" Ernest announced. "She somehow appears if you say her name, and things simply cannot go on like this! We have to figure out how to control her!"

The other animals nodded, but no one said anything.

"Well?" Ernest said testily.

Milly glared at Ernest. "Don't be mad at *us*."

"I'm afraid of her," Gabby said. "She's a bully."

Sir Walter said, "Gabby's right. She scares me."

"None of this is helpful," Ernest said. "She scares me, too, but we're stuck with her, so we need to figure out what to do until Barnabas comes to get her. We need a plan!"

"How about moving her to the aviary?" Milly suggested. "Or to one of the nice outdoor pens? Chickens don't belong in the house!"

Gabby shook her beak. "She won't stay there, Milly. She can go wherever she wants, because she's magic."

"I hate magic, and I hate Malicia!" howled Sir Walter.

"Eeep!" And there she was, in the tack room with them — in their sacred family meeting place.

"Sir Walter! What did I tell you?" grunted Ernest.

"Don't blame the dopey little puppy," Malicia said. "You were gone so long, Ernest, that I wanted to see what you were doing. I got here in time to hear most of it. You were all plotting against me. 'Move her to the aviary,' Milly says. 'Move her to a nice outdoor pen,' she says. Well!! We'll see who gets moved!"

With that, Malicia vanished. *Poof.*

5
That's a Chicken for You

GRAMPA'S FAMILY FELT ANXIOUS for the rest of the day. They had no chance to talk privately until after supper. "When she's asleep," Ernest told Milly, "we'll meet under the dining-room table. Tell Gabby and Sir Walter." Ernest put his head on his blue pillow and made snoring sounds.

Malicia dozed off quickly, tired from her day in the pastures and stuffed with bugs. Her slow, wheezy breathing told Ernest that she was sound asleep, so he tiptoed into the dining room.

When the family had gathered under the table, Ernest said, "You all heard her. She declared war on us."

"I am soooo sorry, Ernest," Milly said. "You had a terrible day." Milly licked his face and moved up to his ears. She believed that a good licking solved most problems. "That bird is just a disaster," Milly said between licks.

"Of course. She's a *chicken,*" Ernest grunted.

Milly kept on licking Ernest, and no one said anything.

"Come on!" Gabby said. "Ernest can't do this all by himself!"

"Do what?" Sir Walter asked, yawning.

"Come up with a plan to control you-know-who! And Sir Walter, do NOT say her name!" Gabby ordered. Then she said, "I'd like to bite her magic head off! I can do it, too. I may be old, but I'm still fast!"

"Grampa can't return a headless chicken to his friend," Ernest observed. "We need a *good* idea, and we need it right now."

But "right now" passed, and so did many more minutes. Sir Walter suggested they toss you-know-who into the pen with the German shepherd that was out in the boarding kennels. The family shook their heads no. Milly offered to take you-know-who upstairs to Grampa's bedroom, stuff her under the pillow, and sit on the pillow. Again the family shook their heads no. Ernest's dependable brain offered nothing, which made him extremely grumpy, so he ended the meeting.

"Keep working on it," he ordered as he stalked off to his bed.

The next morning was Malicia's third day at the Bed and Biscuit. For the first time in Ernest's memory, Rory did not wake anyone with his joyous crowing. At six thirty, after listening to the early news, Grampa came downstairs with Milly, drank his coffee, and left for milking with Milly, Ernest, and Sir Walter.

"Where do you suppose our rooster is?" Grampa said aloud, looking around as he walked. "I'd call for him, but I don't know how to call a rooster."

He stopped then and looked down at Ernest. "But luckily we have Mr. Super Snout! Ernest, you can do it. Go find Rory." He gestured all over the property. "Find Rory," he said again.

"Wrunk," Ernest replied, veering off toward the woods. He caught no scent of the rooster there or behind the barn or in the barnyard. How annoying! He would have to interview the flock of chickens on the far side of the cow pond.

"Where's your chief?" Ernest asked the scruffy old white hen.

For once the old white hen didn't give him a hard time. "We don't know," she replied, "and we're worried. Yesterday a hawk nearly got Wilhelmina, poor dear. That would never have happened if Rory had been with us! Did he go on vacation? Do you know where he is? I mean, we really—"

"There, there," Ernest said, hoping she would shut her beak. "I am looking for him, and I'll let you know when I find him." He trotted off toward the pastures, snout on the ground. In the pasture closest to the barn, he found Malicia, bug hunting.

"What are you doing here?" she asked him.

"Hunting for Rory. He's missing."

"Good. It was nice and quiet this morning, the way it should be." She snapped up a slow beetle.

Ernest said, "Here in the country, we like our roosters. They protect our hens from foxes and hawks and feral dogs, so we listen to their crowing."

"What a price to pay." Malicia shuddered.

Ernest thought of the many kinds of food he loved that came from chickens. "It's a small price," he said. "It's worth it to protect our hens who lay eggs. I love omelets. Have you ever had a cheese omelet?"

"You big booby! Chickens don't eat eggs. Those are our children! Now get lost!"

Head low, Ernest trotted over to the fence, where there were many bushes. He flopped down in the shade between two bushes and grunted in sorrow for his predicament.

"Ernest?" said the larger bush on the left.

Ernest poked his snout into the bush. "Rory! We missed you!"

"You did? Really?"

"Of course! We depend on you. The hens need you!"

"Just forget you saw me. I'm hiding. I lost some tail feathers and I look awful."

Oh, great, thought Ernest. *A typical macho rooster with a self-esteem problem. He's too embarrassed to admit that a teeny chicken got the best of him.* In his most chipper voice, he cried, "We don't care about tail feathers! They'll grow back. We miss your nice crowing." *Well, sort of,* Ernest thought.

"You do? Really?" Rory sounded more upbeat.

"Really! Now I'm going to tell the hens that you're okay and will be back with them soon. You will, won't you?"

"Not for a while," Rory said. "I look ridiculous."

"But a hawk nearly got Wilhelmina yesterday because you weren't there to scare him off!"

Rory's eyes glazed over, and his reddish-brown beak drooped. Then, raising his head, he said, "All right, but you keep that vicious little Silkie away from me and my hens."

"Merowr?" cried Milly, trotting through the deep grass. "Ernest? Did you find him?"

"Over here!" he replied.

Milly picked up her pace. Several yards behind her was Sir Walter, a black dot popping up and down in grass that was as tall as he was. Off and on he cried, "Yarp!" to tell Milly where he was.

Rory was flattered by all the attention. "Thank you for looking for me. What's wrong with that dinky little chicken, anyway? What's her name . . . Malicia?"

"Yarp! Yarp!" Sir Walter barked frantically in warning.

He was too late. Malicia appeared, looking both mean and mad. "You'd better have a darn good reason for summoning me!" she snapped.

Lifting her feathery wings ever so slightly, she edged toward Milly. A few silver stars danced in the air, and Milly went "Aaack!" as her mouth filled with Rhode Island Red tail feathers.

"Oh, no!" cried Ernest.

Wild-eyed, Rory slipped into the bushes where he was hidden.

At the same time, drawn by Sir Walter's barking, Grampa came striding across the grass with Gabby on his shoulder. "What is it, laddie? Did you find Rory?"

"BAD CHICKEN!" screeched Gabby.

Sir Walter hid behind Ernest.

"Milly!" A furious Grampa bent down and picked her up, his eyes on the feathers in her mouth. "What have you done?"

"Chip, chip, chip!" went Malicia.

6

The Doo Incident

MALICIA CHEERED as she danced around Milly in the pasture. "Chip, chip! That's what you get for plotting against me!"

Sir Walter ran in yipping circles around Grampa. He popped up in the air and kept on yipping.

"OINK!" Ernest thrust his snout at Malicia. "Fix it! Right now!"

Grampa kept trying to remove Rory's tail feathers from Milly's mouth, where they seemed to be stuck. "Dangit, Milly, what's the matter with you? It's not like you to torment Rory! Let go of these feathers!"

Malicia started to hop-skip away, but Ernest oinked right behind her. "I said *fix it!*"

"Oh, all right," she said. With a wave of her wing, the feathers fell out of Milly's mouth and Malicia vanished — all in less than a second.

"Mew?" Milly cried low, a pitiful sound.

Gabby lit on Grampa's shoulder and hollered into his ear, "Baaad CHICKEN," meaning Malicia, of course. "Fried chicken! Chicken noodle soup! Chicken à la king! Yum, yum!"

"I don't know what food has to do with all of this!" Grampa snapped. He put an exploratory finger in Milly's mouth, making sure she had no more feathers. "All right, there you go," he said, putting her down. "I suppose you and Rory got into a fight or something, but no more, hear me? No more fighting!"

Milly shot away from him, racing out of the field. "Don't go away mad," Grampa called after her. "Now where's my poor tail-less rooster?" He looked around for Rory, but Rory was silent and well hidden.

Ernest suspected that Milly would hide in the hayloft. She was hurting, and the barn had always been her refuge. *I hate that sneaky, spoiled, rotten, evil chicken,* he fumed. *I don't care if we are supposed to look out for her—I hate her.*

Gabby resumed yelling in Grampa's ear. "Chicken Alfredo! Chicken chow mein! Chicken fricassee!"

"Oh, for heaven's sake!" Grampa pulled Gabby off his shoulder, set her on the top fence rail, and headed toward the house.

Sir Walter threw back his head and howled the howl that only a Scottie can howl.

"Come on, everybody," Ernest said. "Let's go find Milly. We can worry about you-know-who later." He led them in a quick jog toward the barn. In its broad, open doorway he said, "Quiet now. Milly's probably up in the haymow, so let's just tiptoe in here."

Milly stuck her head over the edge of the upper barn floor, where the hay and straw were kept. "You call that a tiptoe?" she said.

"I'm having a bad day!" Ernest retorted.

"Ffffft! You think YOU are having a bad day?"

In his calmest voice Ernest said, "We have to use our heads here, Milly. We just need a plan to manage you-know-who . . . and Grampa will figure out what's going on here, you wait and see!"

"Oh, I plan to wait . . . *right here*. I've never been so insulted in my life! The idea that I would bite Rory's tail feathers. . . ." Milly ranted on and on.

When she paused to breathe, Ernest jumped in. "I agree with you! We're going now, but we'll be back. Just take a nice nap."

"Ffffft! Those who are wrongly accused do not sleep!"

Back at the house, Grampa had set out lunch for everyone. He was muttering, so his family knew he was upset. Normally, he whistled. Before they gathered to eat, he called out the kitchen door, "Here, Milly! Here, kitty, kitty, kitty!"

Of course, Milly did not come to the house — not then, not that afternoon, and not that evening. Before bedtime Grampa walked all over the property calling her. He gave up at ten o'clock and went to bed without his cat.

At dawn the next morning, a very soft "Rooo!" floated in the air.

Ernest raised his head, and there it was again. "Rooo!" But no more. Even so, Rory's attempt to crow lifted Ernest's spirits, and he sat up with a determined bounce. "This is a new day!" he announced to everyone in the kitchen. Surely today his dependable brain would produce a brilliant idea for managing Malicia.

When Grampa came downstairs, Ernest and Sir Walter were waiting for him. "Maybe Milly will show up in the barn," Grampa said, grabbing a hasty swig of coffee and his red cap.

Gabby leaned forward on her curtain rod and yelled down at Malicia, who was still on her perch, trying to sleep. "Chicken casserole! Rotisserie chicken! Chicken salad!"

This time Grampa laughed. He stroked Malicia's velvety feathers and said, "Don't let Gabby pick on you, chickabiddy. She's getting older, you know."

Gabby did a dance of anger on her perch and ground her bill—a dreadful sound—but she was too incensed to say anything.

Grampa adjusted his cap, called Gabby down to his shoulder, and went out the door with Ernest and Sir Walter. "You are very brave,

Gabby," Sir Walter said on their way to the barn. "I'm afraid that you-know-who would magic me if I talked like that."

"Right," said Ernest. *Odd,* he thought, *that Malicia has not punished Gabby for her taunts about chicken being tasty food.* He remembered the other times Gabby had suggested various ways of eating chicken. Of course, Grampa had always been right there. *Aha! There's a promising line of thought.*

That morning Grampa alternately milked cows and called for his cat, who surely heard him, yet she never appeared. Ernest carried milk pails again while Sir Walter ran around getting in trouble. He loved digging into a bale of hay or straw, which made a big mess. By the time they went back to the house, Grampa had scolded him, and all of them were on edge.

Gabby began hunting crumbs under the kitchen table, part of her morning routine, while Malicia still slept soundly on her perch.

Grampa slammed the skillet onto the stove.

"Maybe I need a vacation like Malicia and Barnabas! If it isn't one thing, it's another. Darn Milly! There's nothing like an independent cat to drive a man crazy!"

Malicia came awake with a jerk, ruffling her feathers indignantly. She stared blackly at Grampa, but he didn't even look her way. While he banged skillets and silverware, she vanished in a shower of silver stars.

As she disappeared, Gabby called out, "Chicken potpie! Chinese chicken and rice —"

Grampa turned away from the stove and looked down at her. "Gabby! Why did you do that on my nice floor instead of on your papers?" He pointed at a large pile of bird doo right behind her.

"Wrraack!" Gabby cried, flying wildly upward. "Ernest! Red alert! Red alert! Emergency! BAAAD CHICKEN!"

"Yarp! Yarp!" Sir Walter barked his way around the kitchen as Gabby crumpled into a pile of feathers on the floor.

Ernest ordered himself to be brilliant — right away. He knew that Gabby would never make a mess on the floor, so this was more of Malicia's troublemaking. *Leave it to a chicken,* he thought bitterly.

Lacking a great idea, Ernest stood beneath Malicia's perch and grunted loudly, "It's this chicken! It's all the fault of this evil chicken!" *Oh hear me, hear me and understand!* he begged silently.

An anguished Gabby looked up at Grampa and cried, "Good Gabby! Welcome to the Bed and Biscuit! Pretty girl! Pretty girl!"

"Yarp! Yarp!"

"Oink! Oink! EEEEEE!" from Ernest.

Engulfed in pandemonium, Grampa cried, "Ye gods, I must be losing my mind!" But of course, he got busy cleaning up the bird doo. "Gabby," he asked, "are you getting back at me because I said you were growing old? I am, too, and look at me! I've never been better!"

Gabby was so mad she could only clack her beak. After making as much noise as possible, she went behind the old iron woodstove, where only bugs or a very small animal could go. There, she was silent.

Grampa cleared away breakfast, shook out the tablecloth, and swept his kitchen floor. He whistled determinedly, filling the room with "Waltzing Matilda," Gabby's favorite song.

When he finished, he peered into the dim area behind the stove. "It's dirty back there," he said. "My grandmother cleaned it, but no one else ever has. Come on out, Gabby. I forgive you. You can help Ernest and Sir Walter with chores this morning. Come on!"

Gabby said, "Chicken cutlets! Chicken Kiev! BOILED CHICKEN!" and stayed right where she was.

Grampa put the broom away. "Okay, Ernest, Sir Walter, let's go. Time waits for no man . . . or pig . . . or puppy!" He held the door open for Ernest. Sir Walter pawed at his pants until Grampa picked him up.

Ernest's brain churned all morning while they cleaned the few kennels that held a boarding dog or cat. *This is Malicia's fourth day,* he thought, *and already she's attacked Rory, the cows, Milly, and now Gabby—twice! I think she picks on us for fun! If only Grampa knew what's been going on!*

7

Don't Make Her Mad

LUCKILY FOR GRAMPA'S FAMILY, Malicia was hunting bugs in the near pasture, so the rest of that day was calm. Grampa called for Milly off and on, but she stayed in the hayloft, while Gabby remained behind the old stove.

Only two attended the family meeting under the dining-room table that evening. Head down, Sir Walter told Ernest, "I'm no good to you. I'm just a puppy and I'm scared. I never met a witch-chicken before."

"Don't be too hard on yourself," Ernest replied. "You said something important this morning—about how brave Gabby was. The answer to our problem is in that idea . . . somewhere."

"Too bad we don't have magic," the puppy said. "Then we could put some spells on *her*! See how *she* likes it!"

Ernest mumbled *"Mmm"* because he was busy thinking.

"Ernest?"

"I'm thinking!"

Sir Walter's muzzle jutted forward. "Hey! I'm trying to help!"

"Sorry," Ernest said instantly, nuzzling the small dog. "This is all making me very grumpy. My brain is not working properly, either. I should have had a good idea by now!"

"It's okay. We can count on you. That's what Milly and Gabby always say." Sir Walter sat in front of Ernest and oozed admiration.

Ernest felt his burden of responsibility settle more heavily on his heart. *They are all counting on me,* he thought. *But we don't have any magic like Malicia! We can't appear and disappear whenever we want. . . .*

"Wait a minute," he said out loud. "Whenever we *want*!"

The puppy looked confused. "What are you thinking?"

"I'm wondering if you-know-who is always in control of her magic. Remember when Rory said her name and she came immediately? But she was mad. She said we had 'summoned' her. So . . . that gives me an idea."

Sir Walter hopped to his feet, tail wagging. "Tell me! Tell me!"

"I will, when I've figured it all out. And maybe I'll have a chance to tell you-know-who a few important things. Think about it, Sir Walter. Did she give us a chance to be friends? No. Does she play and enjoy life? No. She just hops around all touchy and irritable. It's as if she's looking for an insult so she can zap somebody! She needs a *good lecture,* if you ask me!"

By now, the puppy had begun to doze off. He yawned and said, "Can we go to bed now? Grampa always says, 'Let's sleep on it,' remember?"

Even before daylight the next morning, Malicia's fifth day at the Bed and Biscuit, Rory sounded off. "Racka, ROOO!" crowed the mighty Rhode Island Red. "ROOO!" he added a bit later.

From her perch Malicia said, "Stupid rooster! He hasn't learned a thing! I have a mind to go back out there and —"

Sir Walter barked into Ernest's ear. "Wake up! She's going after Rory again!"

Ernest sat up abruptly. He glared across the room at the tiny silver hen fidgeting on her perch. *Of all the boarders we've ever had,* he thought, *this one is the biggest pain.*

Gathering all of his patience as the Genial Host, Ernest said, "Rory is just doing his job, Malicia, remember? Maybe a fox is out there and Rory's protecting Grampa's chickens."

"A fox?"

"Yes. They're fast and they love to eat little chickens. So if I were you, I'd stay in here where it's safe and go back to sleep."

"All you ever do is lecture!" grumbled Malicia. But she closed her eyes and sat still.

"A fox? Really?" Sir Walter asked.

"Shhh. I made it up. Go back to sleep!"

Sometime later, Grampa came downstairs as usual and made coffee. While it brewed, he greeted Gabby, still sulking behind the woodstove. When she said nothing, he went to the porch to call for his cat. He was a quiet man that morning, and Ernest felt sorry for him.

"Come on, boys," Grampa said, shrugging on his jacket. "The cows are calling." On his way to the door, he ruffled Malicia's feathers and stroked her head. "You're a sweet little thing," he said. "I'm sorry my animals have caused such a fuss lately." Shaking his head, he stepped out onto the porch ahead of Ernest and Sir Walter.

"YARP!" went Sir Walter, so angry that he forgot his fear. "She's not sweet! She's more trouble than any animal I've ever known! YARP! YARP!"

Ernest shook all over. "Hush! Don't make you-know-who mad!"

But he was too late. Malicia waved her wings, tiny silver stars swirled briefly, and the puppy was hurled into a barking fit. He startled Grampa by jumping out onto the porch, barking much louder than normal—more barks per minute, too. He leaped up and down while he did it. The more he barked, the hoarser he got. His eyes bulged out of his head.

"Sir Walter!" Grampa said. "Stop that!" Of course, nothing Grampa said made any difference.

"YARP! YARP!"

Grampa picked him up and scolded him, but still Sir Walter barked. He couldn't help it.

Ernest advanced on Malicia, who'd come to the porch to enjoy the spectacle and had forgotten to disappear. "Fix it right now!" he grunted. "He's just a baby! Do you always pick on babies?"

"He has a rude mouth!" Malicia snapped.

"Sometimes," Ernest acknowledged, "but he's a puppy. Go on, now, and make him normal again!"

"You're no fun at all, Ernest! Where's your sense of humor?" But when he moved menacingly toward her, she relented. She waved a wing in the puppy's direction and vanished.

Sir Walter drooped, limp and exhausted, in Grampa's arms. He closed his eyes and panted feebly.

"Of all things," Grampa said, clearly mystified. "That was a fit if ever I saw one. I'm putting you in my office for a while, laddie, until I'm sure you're all right."

With a disgruntled Ernest alongside, Grampa strode to his office, where he checked the puppy's heartbeat. He took his temperature, listened to his lungs, and felt him all over. He tucked him into a roomy cage and set it next to his desk.

"Here's some water, fella. I'll be back with breakfast after milking. Come along, Ernest, we're running late."

Sir Walter howled.

"Just rest," Ernest told him. "Remember what we talked about earlier? I'm working on a good idea, and I'll tell you as soon as I can."

8
Poor Professor Pig

AFTER MILKING, Ernest and Grampa went back to the house as usual. While Grampa worked indoors to separate all those gallons of milk from the cream, Ernest stayed outdoors. He needed a calm, restful place and time to develop his plan.

The best place for both was in his personal pig shower beside the porch steps. He stood on the sparkly white stones, pulled the chain, and grunted with pleasure as the water rained down. He opened his mouth for a drink, then simply stood still, enjoying the gift of clean water.

For some time he talked to his brain. *We need a plan that will work,* he said. *We have to get her under control! For sure, whatever we do has to be where Grampa will see it.* He thought about those words: *whatever we do.*

Yes, he decided, *the key to this is* we. *If we all work together, that will give us courage. Together we can be brave, like Sir Walter said, and we will have to be brave to take on Malicia and her magic.* Ernest paused, reflecting on the progress of his thoughts. He waggled his ears so that the water would wash them thoroughly, inside and out.

We need Grampa to see all of it, Ernest concluded, *the way* we *have. So if Malicia wants to freeze us or have us eat feathers or make us bark, we'll just have to suffer. Grampa will see it and . . .*

"Enough, Ernest!" Grampa hollered from his office. "Leave some water in the well for the rest of us!"

Ernest yanked the chain that turned off the water. The late autumn sun shone down upon him as he stood there drying, and for the first time in days he felt hopeful.

"I always heard that pigs were dirty," Malicia said.

There she was, sitting on a porch step, only inches from his snout.

"You heard wrong," he said shortly. "All pigs love clean water if they can get it. And sweet grass. Shady houses to raise piglets in. Healthy pastures for rooting. Grampa has a saying about pigs: 'Root or die.' That's true! We get valuable minerals from the soil by rooting."

Malicia closed her eyes. "Quit lecturing!"

"Hey! I live here, remember? I can talk all I want!" Too late, Ernest realized his mistake.

The tiny silver stars swirled, Malicia's wings waved, and Ernest felt a weird tingling in his throat. He grunted at Malicia, only it wasn't a grunt. It was a bird's cheep.

"Cheep! Cheeep!" he said. Then, furiously, "CHEEP! CHEEEP!!"

Gabby tore out onto the porch. "What in—?"

Malicia rolled around on the step. "Chip, chip!" she laughed. "Oh, I am so clever! I just astound myself!"

Gabby flew in circles above Ernest's head. "Be calm, Ernest. We'll think of something!"

"Not with your birdbrain! Chip, chip, chip!" tittered Malicia.

"CHEEP! CHEEEP!" Ernest roared. Now his head felt hard and cold. So did his body. He told his feet to move, but they felt like frozen lumps — rooted in the stones of his shower floor. All he could do was cheep like some grotesque bird.

"Hold on, Ernest!" Gabby cried. "Grampa's coming!"

Malicia quit cackling and stood up. She waved one wing at Ernest and vanished.

Ernest shook himself all over and gave a few test oinks. *Ah, thank goodness, I am me again! That was* terrifying. *Malicia, you're going to be sorry! Oh, great corn dogs, are you going to be sorry!*

By late afternoon, Grampa felt that Sir Walter was all right. With Ernest's anxious supervision, he opened the puppy's cage. Sir Walter charged out, ready to bark, but instead he closed his mouth and whimpered. Grampa chuckled and picked him up. "After this morning, you might never bark again, right, laddie?"

Sir Walter licked Grampa's face.

Outside, Grampa put him in the grass beside Ernest. "Better run off some energy. It's getting dark already." He went to the house to work on supper while Sir Walter dashed up and down the grassy square.

When at last the puppy flopped down, panting, Ernest sat beside him. "Okay, pay attention. It's tonight."

"What's tonight?"

"Tonight, after supper, is when we're going to convince you-know-who to behave herself."

9
So Many Stars

"TONIGHT?" SIR WALTER YELPED. "We're doing it tonight?" Then he tensed up. "*What* are we doing?"

"Well," Ernest said, "we need to show her we will not be trifled with! She will see how a real family acts! How good triumphs over evil! How—"

"Ernest? What are you going to *do*?"

"It's not just me. It's *all of us.* We are all going to demonstrate how we feel about the way she's been treating us. After tonight she will know exactly what we think about her brand of magic! Yes, sir! After all, there's good magic, like rabbits popping out of hats, and there's bad mag—"

"Ernest! What are we going to DO?"

"I've just been telling you!"

"Not exactly." Sir Walter scratched behind his left ear.

"Well, I will tell you — Milly and Gabby, too. Let's go get them."

Sir Walter stayed close to Ernest as they went to the barn to talk Milly into coming home. In closing, Ernest said, "We need your help, Milly. All of us have to show Grampa what's really been happening. Then he'll know you didn't pull out Rory's tail feathers."

"He hasn't apologized to me yet!" Milly's emerald eyes glittered.

"He couldn't! He doesn't know where you are!"

Milly sat down. "Oh, all right, but this better be a good idea, Ernest!"

"It is. In fact, it may be a brilliant idea. But we must plan our exposé of you-know-who carefully."

"What's an 'exposé'?"

"It's an exposure — showing something bad that has been going on in secret. We are staging an exposé of a chicken gone wrong! We need to do it well so that Grampa understands, and these things take planning!"

"Let's go home. I'm hungry," said Sir Walter.

"Food can wait! Go get Gabby!" Ernest ordered.

In only a few minutes, all four of Grampa's animals huddled in a circle in the tack room. Ernest's explanation of his plan was brief. It was a simple plan, after all. "If we are brave, this should work," he said at the end. "He'll see the stars and us, and that should do it."

"I can be brave," Sir Walter said, his voice barely quivering.

"Atta boy!" said Gabby. "No scrawny little chicken is going to get the better of us!"

Milly swished her tail vigorously back and forth. "Let's go! I can't wait for Grampa to see this and figure out what an idiot he's been!"

Ernest blinked. "I've never heard you talk like that!"

"That's because I'm so sweet and loving — just not right now. Come on, everybody."

When they came through the pet door, one after another, Grampa jumped up from his chair and grabbed Milly. He spoke loving words in her ear, but Milly squirmed to get away.

"Hmm. Still mad at me, aren't you?" He turned to his mynah bird. "How about you, Gabby?" Grampa said.

Gabby flew to the back of the chair next to Grampa and screeched, "BAAAD CHICKEN!"

"I'll give you an extra pear if you stop that," Grampa told her.

He bent down to stroke Malicia's feathers. "Ignore her, sweetie. You're a *good chicken*." Malicia was gobbling Gabby's crumbs on the floor by his chair and paid him no attention.

As the supper hour proceeded, Grampa looked up from his newspaper now and then to smile at Milly and Gabby. The ringing phone startled everyone.

"Bed and Biscuit. Dr. Bender speaking." Grampa held the receiver away from his ear as Barnabas's powerful voice greeted him and asked about his chicken.

"Oh, she's dandy," Grampa said. "She's gained four ounces already! That's a lot on a tiny bird. She loves our bugs!" He was quiet, listening, then said, "Lonely? How could she be lonely here? We're all keeping an eye on her. How's your trip going?"

Malicia had stopped eating to listen to the phone conversation.

"We're doing fine, Barnabas. Come home when you're ready." Grampa hung up the phone and took his paper to the family room.

Ernest gave everyone a meaningful glance and said, "Now. Take your battle stations."

Gabby flew into the family room and perched on the arm of the couch, close to Grampa. Sir Walter trotted to the corner of the kitchen on the left side of the porch door, while Milly hopped into Grampa's big chair on the right side of the door. Ernest sat in front of his bed, which meant he was all the way across the kitchen from the door.

They were at their posts, so Ernest said, "Hey, Malicia, how's it going?"

"Eeep!" As before, Malicia came instantly at the sound of her name. "Ernest! Can't you see I'm eating? What's the matter with you?"

From Grampa's big chair, Milly called, "Malicia! Over here! You missed a crumb!"

"Eeep!" Malicia appeared in front of the chair. "A crumb? You called me over here for one measly crumb?"

Gabby whistled from the family room. "Hoo, hoo, Malicia! Over here!"

"EEEP!" Malicia landed next to Gabby on the sofa arm. By now she was breathing hard. "If I hear my name one more time, I'll— "

"Oh, yeah? What'll you do, Malicia? Mean-ee Malicia! Mean-ee Malicia!" By the kitchen door, Sir Walter braced himself in a tough-dog stance, but his short legs were shaking.

"EEEP!" Silver stars flashed and crackled as Malicia appeared beside Sir Walter. With a wave of her wing, all of Sir Walter began shaking. His head bobbed, his legs jerked, his tail whipped from one side to the other, and he blinked constantly.

Grampa looked up from his paper.

"In here, Malicia!" cried Gabby from the family room. "There's a cricket by the fireplace."

"EEEP!" Stars popped and snapped as Malicia landed by Gabby. "I'll give you a cricket!" Malicia cried, waving her wings wildly. Crickets appeared everywhere — on the furniture, in the fireplace, on Gabby's head — all chirping noisily.

Grampa shook his head and began to stand up. "What the — "

Ernest took a deep breath. "Malicia! I'd like a word with you."

"EEEEP!" Stars exploded all around Ernest as Malicia appeared. "Stop it! All of you, stop it! I never want to hear another word from any of you!" She whirled in a circle, frantically waving her wings.

Ernest saw Milly, Gabby, and Sir Walter dropping to the floor in rigid shapes like statues. He felt his own legs splay out in all directions, with his head and snout stretched out. *She's done it now!* he thought. *I can't move!*

"Great heavens! MALICIA!" cried Grampa, stamping one foot.

"EEEEP!" shrieked Malicia as she appeared before Grampa. Instantly, she blitzed the room with glittering stars that hissed and sizzled like miniature firecrackers. Smoke filled the air.

Grampa clapped his hands loudly and said, "MALICIA! Stop all of this immediately!"

In an eyeblink, Malicia's wings waved in a circle, banishing the crickets, undoing all of the magic. She collapsed in a small gray pile of feathers on the floor. The stars fizzled and went out, leaving an eerie silence.

10
A Power Outage

ERNEST TOOK A deep, grateful breath and moved his legs. He shifted his hooves, waggled his curly tail, and stood up. Gabby, Milly, and the puppy were all making similar motions. Ernest went to Grampa and put his snout on Grampa's knee. "Wrunk?" he said softly. He gazed into Grampa's eyes and ached for him to understand.

Grampa rubbed his face as if waking from a heavy sleep. He reached out and put one quivering hand on Ernest's head. He patted and patted, and Ernest knew they had made themselves understood. *As humans go,* Ernest thought, *this one is the champion.*

Grampa reached down and picked up the tiny Silkie.

"Eeeep," went Malicia, sounding weak and pitiful for the first time.

"Well, well! Aren't you something! *Baaaad chicken* is right! I should have listened to Gabby."

"Hallelujah!" said Gabby, dredging up one of her favorite long words.

"Eeep," Malicia repeated, giving her impression of a dying chicken.

"I'm not fooled," Grampa told her.

Having looked around and seen that his family appeared normal, he said, "Be right back, troops." He wrapped Malicia in a towel to keep out the evening chill and went outdoors with her in his arms. He returned in a few minutes with Malicia inside her own cage. While his family watched, he put food and water in the cage, draped the towel over it, and set it in the corner farthest from Ernest's bed.

Grampa sat down and drummed his fingers on the table. "Life is never dull around here," he said to no one in particular. "Here I thought we were all hunky-dory, and all the time you . . . you bad chicken, you!" He shook his finger at Malicia's cage. "I suppose I'd better call Barnabas."

Grampa got busy with his phone call, and Ernest moseyed over to Malicia's cage. He couldn't help himself. He was a naturally thoughtful pig. "Are you all right?" he asked.

"No. I was the victim of a mob attack."

"You drove us to it. We'll do it again if you keep picking on us."

"Don't worry. You were right when you said I was wasting my magic on small things. I tried to get out of this cage and I can't do it. My career is over."

Ernest was dumbfounded. *I wonder if I can just say things and they'll come true?* he thought. *Maybe I have a strange power that is only now revealing itself!* Then his brain took over. *Get hold of yourself, Ernest! You are a brilliant mini-pig, and that's it.*

He gave Malicia a closer look. She seemed greatly subdued — for now, anyway. "I wouldn't worry," he said. "You'll probably be back to normal tomorrow, after you've rested."

They both listened as Grampa said good-bye to his friend. "It's okay. We can talk tomorrow when you have more time." Grampa then herded his family to the brown corduroy sofa in the family room, where Gabby perched on his shoulder. Milly sat on his right, Sir Walter on his left. Ernest sat on the rug, touching Grampa's leg. He looked expectantly at Grampa, who was going to lead what he called a family discussion. Grampa always did the talking, of course.

But not tonight. In a near whisper, Gabby said, "Baaad chicken."

A smile lit Grampa's face. "Yes, ma'am! She played me for a sucker, didn't she?" He stroked Gabby's head, then began petting his cat. "All this time I though you folks were misbehaving, when it was that little chicken's fault every time. I had no idea what she could do." He massaged Sir Walter's back.

Grampa continued loving his animals. "I nearly went crazy just now when I saw all of you under some kind of . . . spell! And I can't even tell anyone about it except Barnabas! No one else would believe me."

Gabby rubbed her beak on Grampa's face and said, "Roast chicken?"

"Hold on," he said, smiling. "If Barnabas can tell me how to work with her, we'll have her show us some *good* magic tomorrow. We really need to start over with this chicken."

We need to send this chicken home! Ernest thought. And then his dependable brain said, *On the other hand, a fresh start is always a good idea.*

Now his brain hummed with ideas. *Maybe this time she could make the cows sing. Turn Gabby into a pterodactyl. Show graceful Milly how to dance. Help Sir Walter dig a hole the size of our biggest cow pond.*

As for me, he thought, *I want cornbread for lunch every day.*

Author's Note

SILKIE BANTAM CHICKENS

Few chickens are as appealing or as good-tempered as the unique breed known as Silkies. (Malicia is an exception!) Like other bantam chickens, Silkies are small, with cocks weighing about four pounds and hens weighing about three pounds. Unlike other chickens, which have four toes, Silkies have five toes on each foot. Their skin and bones are dark slate blue, a trait most people find off-putting, so they rarely appear on menus.

The Chinese name for them is *wu gu ji,* which means "black-boned chicken." Peek at their ears, and you'll find turquoise earlobes. Despite these unique qualities, Silkies are not "magic" in any way, except for the magical appeal of their waggling fluffy bustles as they pace across the barnyard.

They don't live longer than other chickens, either, despite what Barnabas claims about Malicia's age. Most pet chickens can live twelve to fifteen years if they're well protected. The normal farm chicken, often the victim of predators, typically lives anywhere from five to ten years.

The first record of Silkie bantam chickens comes from the explorer Marco Polo, who journeyed in the Far East in the thirteenth century. He wrote about seeing "chickens with hair like cats that lay the best of eggs." Their white or light brown eggs are delicious, but so tiny that it takes four of them to equal a typical large egg. Silkie hens love to sit on their nests and hatch their eggs. They don't even care if the eggs are not their own!

Silkies come in several colors: white, black, blue, buff, gray, partridge (brownish), splash (gray and white mixed) — even lavender (vaguely bluish white). Another variety is the bearded Silkie, with even more feathers, especially around the head. Because they're so cute and so friendly, Silkies are popular pets. People who never liked chickens before fall in love with their Silkies.

Join Ernest the mini-pig for more adventures at the Bed & Biscuit!

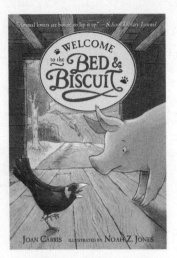 

Welcome to the Bed & Biscuit

Wild Times at the Bed & Biscuit

Joan Carris
illustrated by Noah Z. Jones

What do a Scottish puppy, a Canada goose, a cranky muskrat, and two starving fox kits have in common? They all disrupt Ernest's peaceful life at the animal boardinghouse! Will he be able to keep his friends together — and keep them from going *too* wild?